KATIE AND THE MONA·LISA

James Mayhew

ORCHARD BOOKS

For my wife
Maria Antonietta De Salve
who has a lovely smile

For more about the Mona Lisa and Italian Renaissance painters turn to the end of the book.

ORCHARD BOOKS
338 Euston Road, London NW1 3BH
Orchard Books Australia
Level 17/207 Kent Street, Sydney, NSW 2000

First published in 1998 by Orchard Books
First published in paperback in 1999

Text and illustrations © James Mayhew 1998

The right of James Mayhew to be identified as author and illustrator
of this work has been asserted by him in accordance with the
Copyright, Designs and Patents Act, 1988.

A CIP catalogue record for this book is available from the British Library.

ISBN 978 1 86039 706 6

20 19 18 17 16 15 14 13

Printed in China

Orchard Books is a division of Hachette Children's Books
an Hachette UK company.

www.hachette.co.uk

Katie and her grandma often went to the gallery on their days out together. Grandma liked to tell Katie all about the famous paintings.

"Which picture do you like best?" asked Grandma.

"*Mona Lisa*," said Katie. "She smiled at me."

"She smiles at everyone," said Grandma. "That's why she's famous."

"What makes her smile?" asked Katie.
"I don't know," said Grandma, resting
on a chair. "Perhaps you should have a
closer look at her."

"*Mona Lisa* by Leonardo da Vinci," said Katie, reading the notice by the painting. "I wish I knew what is making you smile."

"Then come inside, *Bambina*!" said Mona Lisa.

Katie was very surprised. But Grandma was dozing and the gallery was empty. So Katie climbed over the frame and inside the picture.

Mona Lisa was sitting in a grand room with a balcony.

"*Bambina*!" she said. "How lovely to see you. I have not had a visitor for hundreds of years!"

"That's a long time," said Katie. "Don't you get lonely?"

"Yes, very," said Mona Lisa. "I am supposed to smile but I don't feel very happy at all."

Mona Lisa started to look sad. A small tear ran down her cheek and her smile disappeared.

"I'll cheer you up," said Katie, handing her a handkerchief.

"When Leonardo painted me, he asked clowns and musicians to make me smile," said Mona Lisa, blowing her nose.

"Can you dance or sing?"

"I've got a better idea," said Katie. She took Mona Lisa by the hand and very carefully they stepped out of the picture and into the gallery.

"You can meet anyone you like here," said Katie. "I'm sure there is someone who can make you smile again."

They looked at the pictures,
one by one.

At last they stopped in front of
St George and the Dragon by Raphael.

"A knight in shining armour!"
said Mona Lisa. "Can I meet him?"

"If we climb inside," said Katie.

So Mona Lisa gathered up her
long skirts and Katie took her
through the frame.

Saint George was rescuing a beautiful
princess from a fire-breathing dragon. But he
forgot all about her when he saw Mona Lisa.
"Ah! *Bella*!" he said, climbing off his horse.
He kissed Mona Lisa gallantly on the hand.

At once, the dragon ran off and started to chase
the princess again.

"*Mamma mia!*" said Mona Lisa.

"Help, save me!" cried the princess. She leapt
out of the picture, with the dragon flying after her.
Saint George grabbed his lance and dashed
off to the rescue.

"Now I'm all alone again," sighed Mona Lisa.

"Perhaps we can try another picture?" suggested Katie.

They climbed out and walked into another room.

Mona Lisa pointed to a picture by Sandro Botticelli,
called *Primavera*, which means Spring.
"Look at the dancers!" she said. "I'd love to meet them!"
So Katie clambered inside and Mona Lisa followed her.

Katie and Mona Lisa found themselves in an enchanted grove where everyone was dancing. The scent of flowers filled the air.

"Welcome to springtime," said a beautiful woman in a flowery dress. "I am Flora, come with me and taste the oranges!"

Flora helped Katie gather sweet juicy oranges
from the trees whilst Mona Lisa joined in the dance.
"I think I could be happy if I stayed here," she said.

But Katie slipped and fell on to the three dancers. They all ended up on the ground, covered with squashed oranges.

"You have ruined the springtime dance, just wait until we get our hands on you," said the dancers.

"Perhaps it's best if we don't stay," said Katie.

"I think you may be right," sighed Mona Lisa.

They quickly climbed out of the picture
and ran into another room before the three
dancers could catch them.

Mona Lisa saw a picture called *The Lion
of St Mark* by Vittore Carpaccio.

She could see the city of Venice behind the Lion.
"I've always wanted to visit Venice," sighed Mona Lisa.
Katie thought it would be a good place to hide from
the angry dancers. She took Mona Lisa's hand and went
through the frame and into the picture.

The Lion was very friendly.

"Welcome to Venice!" he said.

"There's water everywhere," said Katie. "Is there a flood?"

"Venice was built on the sea," said the Lion. "I shall carry you over the water."

They climbed on the Lion's back, and he opened his beautiful rainbow wings and flew up into the air. Below them, Venice sparkled like silver and gold.

The Lion carried them to the Grand Canal and they got into a boat called a gondola.

The people of Venice waved and sang songs and gave them pasta and ice-cream to eat. Katie wanted to have seconds of everything, but just then she saw that the gondola had sprung a leak.

"My dress will be ruined!" cried Mona Lisa. "What shall we do?"

"I'll fly you back to the picture frame," said the Lion. "Climb on!"

They held on to the Lion's mane and he flew up into the sky.

"I'm slipping off!" yelled Katie, hanging on to one of the Lion's wings.

"Oh, dear," said the Lion, "I think I'm going to... CRASH!"

They flew straight through the frame and fell into the gallery.

"*Mamma mia!*" said Mona Lisa.

There in front of them sat the dragon.

He puffed out clouds of smoke and roared at them.

And behind the dragon stood Saint George and the princess and the three dancers. They all looked very cross indeed.

"Oh dear, what a muddle!" said Katie. "What shall we do?"

Suddenly, the gallery was filled with sweet music.
It was coming from another picture, called *An Angel
with a Lute* painted by a student of Leonardo da Vinci.

The angel came out of his picture and stroked the dragon. He stopped growling, lay down and wagged his tail.

"How clever!" said the princess. "You've tamed him!"

The princess put her belt around his neck and led him proudly back to the picture.

Saint George kissed Mona Lisa's hand once more and followed them.

The angel played on, and
the three graceful dancers smiled
and twirled and skipped happily
back to the orange grove.

The Lion flew back to Venice,
growling a farewell.

"Please can you help Mona Lisa?" said Katie to the angel. "I wanted to make her smile, but everything went wrong."

"She doesn't need my help," said the angel. "Just look!"

And Katie saw that Mona Lisa WAS smiling!

"*Mamma Mia*!" she said. "What an adventure we've had, *Bambina*. Wasn't it fun?"

"Yes it was," said Katie, and they both laughed.

Katie thanked the angel and watched him fly back into his painting.

"Will you be happy in your picture?" Katie said to Mona Lisa.

"I shall think of you and that will make me laugh," she said, climbing through the frame. "Thank you for making me smile again, *Bambina. Addio.*"

"*Addio!*" said Katie.

Katie ran back to her grandma.

"I found out all about Mona Lisa's smile!" said Katie. "But I can't say, you wouldn't believe me."

"I expect you're right," said Grandma. "Now what would you like for supper?"

"Pasta and ice-cream," said Katie. "They're my favourite."

And she smiled a secret smile, just like Mona Lisa.

Mona Lisa and the Italian Renaissance

The paintings in this book were painted during THE RENAISSANCE which means "rebirth' or "new beginning". The Renaissance was a time of great change in which painters and writers and musicians created wonderful works of art and scientists, inventors and explorers started to discover new and wonderful things. The Renaissance started in Italy, and that is where the paintings in this book come from.

Leonardo da Vinci (1452-1519)

Leonardo was an inventor, scientist, mathematician and explorer as well as an artist. The Mona Lisa was one of Leonardo's favourite paintings. Her smile is supposed to be very mysterious. Some people say that Mona Lisa was entertained by clowns and jugglers whilst she posed for the painting and that is what made her smile. The Mona Lisa can be seen in the Louvre Gallery in Paris, France. The picture of the angel was painted by one of Leonardo's students. It is called An Angel with a Lute, and can be seen at The National Gallery in London, England.

Sandro Botticelli (1445-1510)

Botticelli's real name was Alessandro di Mariano dei Filipepi, and he probably took the name Botticelli from the Italian word meaning 'beater of gold' because, when he was young he worked with a goldsmith. Botticelli painted lots of large wall paintings called frescos as well as pictures like the Primavera. You can see the Primavera in the Uffizi Gallery in Florence, Italy.

Raphael (1483-1520)

Raphael's real name was Raphael Sanzio. He studied art under great painters such as Perugino, and Leonardo. Raphael liked to paint scenes from dramatic stories, many of which came from legends and from the Bible. You can see his painting of St George and the Dragon at the National Gallery of Art in Washington D.C., USA.

Vittore Carpaccio (1460-1525/6)

Carpaccio had a great interest in telling stories through his paintings. He is known best for his paintings showing different scenes from one story. Carpaccio lived in Venice and the winged lion in his painting is the symbolic protector of Venice. This painting is still in the Duke's Palace in Venice, Italy to this day.

You will find many other wonderful drawings and paintings by these and other Renaissance artists in galleries all over the world.

Acknowledgements

Mona Lisa by Leonardo da Vinci; Musée d'Louvre; © Photo RMN - R.G. Ojeda An Angel in Red with a Lute by Associate of Leonardo; Reproduced by courtesy of the trustees of the National Gallery, London St. George and the Dragon by Raphael; © Board of Trustees, National Gallery of Art, Washington DC BEN558 Primavera c. 1478 (tempera on panel) by Sandro Botticelli (1444/5-1510) Galleria degli Uffizi, Italy/Bridgeman Art Library, London FTB60402 The Lion of St Mark by Vittore Carpaccio (c. 1460/5-1523/6) Palazzo Ducale, Venice/Bridgeman Art Library, London